THIS IS A BORZOI BOOK PUBLISHED BY ALFRED A. KNOPF
Text copyright © 1967, renewed 1995 by Leo Lionni
Jacket art and interior illustrations copyright © 2021 by Noraeleo, LLC
Illustrated by Leo Lionni and Jan Gerardi

All rights reserved. Published in the United States by Alfred A. Knopf, an imprint of Random House Children's Books, a division of Penguin Random House LLC, New York. Originally published in different form by Pantheon Books, an imprint of Random House Children's Books, New York, in 1967.

Knopf, Borzoi Books, and the colophon are registered trademarks of Penguin Random House LLC.

Visit us on the Web! rhcbooks.com
Educators and librarians, for a variety of teaching tools, visit us at RHTeachersLibrarians.com

Library of Congress Cataloging-in-Publication Data is available upon request.
ISBN 978-0-593-37475-7 (trade) — ISBN 978-0-593-37476-4 (lib. bdg.)

The text of this book is set in 19-point Century Schoolbook.
The illustrations were created using mixed media and digital collage.

MANUFACTURED IN CHINA
November 2021 10 9 8 7 6 5 4 3 2 1

MOUSE
SEASONS

Leo Lionni

Alfred A. Knopf ⚘ New York

Who scatters the snowflakes?

Who melts the ice?

Who spoils the weather?

Who makes it nice?

Who grows the four-leaf clovers in June?

Who dims the daylight?
Who lights the moon?

Four little field mice who live in the sky.
Four little field mice . . . like you and I.

One is the Springmouse
who turns on the showers.

Then comes the Summer who paints in the flowers.

The Fallmouse is next with walnuts and wheat.

And Winter is last . . . with little cold feet.

Aren't we lucky the seasons are four?

Think of a year with one less . . . or one more!